I

DEDICATED TO MY PARENTS IN HEAVEN

Mr. Thomas James DeBose

&

Mrs. Mozelle 'Madea' DeBose

THE BEGINING OF SEASON ONE!
"THE OFFSEASON"

COACH 'EM UP! ™
Is a Registered Trademark

CREDITS:
Cover illustration
Copyright 2020/2021 Jerome DeBose

Cover Design Illustrations by:
Matt Davies for Very Much So.agency
Manchester, UK

Book Design and production by:
Jerome DeBose

Research Assistant
Elaine S.

Book Editing by:
Margaret Joyce

Photography:
Steven Le, TheePhotoNinja.com

DISCLAIMER:
This is a work of fiction!
Names and characters, businesses, places, events, locales, and incidents are either the products of the author's imagination or used in a fictitious manner.
Any resemblance to actual persons, living or dead, or actual events is purely coincidental.

All cast Illustrations are
Computer generated (CGI) photo depictions.
No copyright infringements intended

The Historical YMCA, St. Petersburg, Florida
www.TheEdwardStPete.com

Book Ordering information: www.CoachEmUpSeries.com

Copyright Office registration number: TXu 2-271-235
ISBN: 979-8-987-9858-1-6

2021 First Edition
Conceived, Written and Made in the USA

____

VI

JEROME DEBOSE

_________________ *Cast of Players* _________________

Coach Hasara: Black
Head Coach of the Professional Football Team

Zephyr: Red
Footballer, Wide Receiver on Hasara's team

Candi Rae Hasara: Blue
Daughter of Coach Hasara

Jazlyn: Orange
Friend of Candi Rae, Girlfriend of Marquise B.

Shawna: Purple
Old friend of Candi Rae and Jazlyn

Marquise Brimson: Dk. Grn
Asst. Coach of Hasara, Ex-footballer, Boyfriend of Jazlyn

Clarissa: Pink
Old friend of Coach Hasara

Adam Dumars: Dk. Brn
ESPN News Reporter

Grace Seavers: Lt. Blue
Private Investigator

_______________________ *CEU Intro* _______________________

This Story / Play / Miniseries...
Is written in a colorful 'Pseudo' script form...

All of the characters have a specific color for their dialogue.

Also, each section heading has the characters list at the top,
And characters are in the order of their appearance.

Familiarizing the characters dialogue color and reading in good lighting
makes the entire story more pleasurable!

Thank You for your time of reading this story,
I Hope That You Enjoy...

Jerome DeBose

____

X

______________ *Index Season 1* ______________

(THE END... ZONE)

____

Coach 'Em Up! S1/1

Coach TJ Hasara (Dad) = Blk   Zephyr (Baller) = Red   Candi Rae (Daughter) = Blue

---

(At the Coach's house… as he opens the front door for Zephyr)
Hey Zephyr, come on in..!

Thanks Coach…

Wow that was perfect timing, I just got in from picking up my daughter from the airport, How'r you doing?

I'm good… wow Coach.. Your crib is dope!

I've seen pictures of your place too, looks awfully comfortable as well

You know Coach, a fellow needs a place to rest those aching bones!

I'm sure, hence all of the naked ladies in your pool and hot tub that massages you..

I gotta stay in top physical form!

Yeah, that's actually why I called you over

Because of my physique?

No, because of the allegations that's pending against you…

WHAT ALLEGATIONS?

Apparently a couple of women and their attorney have come forward and
approached the league's office with collaborating testimony…
that you physically assaulted them!

Coach are you serious? Man I've never assaulted anyone!
I don't know anything about that shit Coach, When did this come about…

Moments ago... they are threating to go to the press in the morning!

Oh God... I don't know anything, or haven't heard anything about this until now!

Yeah, their Attny said you took advantage of them at your place, left some marks
and bruises on both of the victims, during two separate incidents...
They have the evidence pics of what they are claiming.

NO WAY!
I was always with my crew, my BOYS are always around.. Always got my back..!

Well at this time they got signed statements from, 'Your BOYS' that say they don't
know where you were at a certain time frame...

Oh hell no!
This some kinda bullshit..!

Na... It's for real man...

Damn, so now what Coach?

First of all, I suggest contacting YOUR Attny.
I got a feeling this isn't going to play out quickly or painlessly..!

Yeah... my Attny.
Damn!

Oh and um, and the team owners had a meeting moments ago also, and they
discussed the negative aspects of the allegations and will be making a formal
statement later today on ESPN...

About what??

About you being released from the team..!

COACH Nooo!

Com'on Zephyr, you know in your heart this is real...
you play with fire, you're bound to get burned!

Well true, but, it's no greater tragedy than for those women to have to
endure what they have!!

I hear you, but unfortunately,
it's not up to me to determine what the outcome may be...
But at this point, I'll also suggest, praying!

Oh okay, I see my neighbor at her mailbox,
I guess the mailman just passed by, I'm expecting an important package,
I need to go get it but I hope she doesn't see me,
she always has these long crazy conversations... ugh!
Excuse me, I'll be right back!

Yes, anyone with a cell phone and internet knows who you are…
But, I'm the coach's daughter, Candi Rae.!

What..?
I know of Kaisha, I didn't know coach had another daughter…

Well, I'm actually the middle daughter, I have a younger sister.

Really, where's she, upstairs?

She's still in the Caribbean with our mom.
We've never really lived with my dad, just visits every now and then…

Wow all of the years that I've followed the coach's career,
and have been on the team, never knew about you two at all…

Well I have a question I've always been curious about.

What's that?

Why do they call you Zephyr?

Really.. Hehe… That was started by a sports writer with the Daily Times!

Why, cause you drank a lot of water..? Lol

Haha.. No, but that's funny…

Ok… then why?

Cause the writer was standing on the sidelines during one of our games, and the
play started and I ran a post route to the end zone really fast, the writer said he
never seen me run pass him, just felt the wind from me going by him so fast…
so he nick named me…

…. Zephyr!!

Yes ma'am... At your service!!

Cool... So that's when you got those sneaker deals!

Yeah Nike jumped on the marketing idea for the kicks,
(The Zephyr Wind) and (The Zephyr Wind 2)
and the new ones due to be released next week... (The Zephyr Fire)!

Dang that's tight, my friend has a pair of the (Z-Wind 2's)... real niice!
I like 'em better than the new Jordan's

Yeah! Thx, I appreciate that... Well I hope Nike doesn't drop me before
we can introduce them next week...

What? Why would they drop you?

Oh my god... it's embarrassing.

Why, what's going on?

Your dad... Coach just informed me that, um...

It's okay, you can talk to me... or not.
But I know it's something really heavy on you and my dad, cause I had never
seen him crying before, that was just as he picked me up from the airport.

 REALLY?

Yeah, he's hurt.. I know this game, this sport is a business...
but to my dad, all of you guys are human to him,
each one of you guys he truly cares about... So what ever it is, this is special..!

Wow... probably cause he never had any sons..?

More than that, we had a little brother that was still born, mom said dad blamed
her and he never got over it!

Yeah, so is that when she left and went back to the Caribbean?

Yeah.. Dad has been alone ever since…
His team is his boys… Or his boys are his team!

Wow!!

That's why his heart is always into it, it's not just a game to him!

Yes Ms. Richmond… I think aliens could have infected the earth with Covid
to get rid of all humans…

OMG! They need to do a psych evaluation on that lady…

Oh hey baby, I see you've met Zephyr…

Yes daddy!

Coach I never knew you have three lovely daughters…

Yes I have three daughters, and I believe they have great lives now,
and great futures ahead of them!

Well coach you're sounding a little protective yourself… I'm no threat,
don't believe all that crap from the league's office!

All of what crap??

Nothing baby, this doesn't concern you… It's sports business

Well I'm getting the feeling it's far more than you guys wanna discuss, at least in
front of me

Actually that's true… Can you please excuse us…

Okay daddy, but remember… You've always told us that we should be open with you about our lives… I know this may be business, but if it really concerns you as a person, please, don't keep me in the dark!

Ok baby, I promise!

I'll be upstairs, my friend Jazlyn is coming over in a few, were going to go hangout for a little while, I haven't seen her in years!

(As his daughter leaves to go upstairs)

Nice meeting you… Candi Rae!!

Nice to have met you… Mr. Wind!! (Hehe)

Com'on Zeph let's go to the kitchen.

Whasup??

Candi's friend will be here soon and we could use a little privacy…
And besides, I'm kinda hungry I haven't eaten all day

Yeah Coach this whole situation, I don't know what to think.. just doesn't add up

(The Coach and Zephyr walk towards the kitchen)
 I need a sandwich or something.. We can talk in there.

TO BE CONTINUED

Coach 'Em Up! S1/2

Candi Rae Hasara (Daughter) = Blue   Jazlyn (Candi's friend) = Orange

---

Coach TJ Hasara (Dad) = Blk   Zephyr (Baller) = Red

(The door bell rings, Candi Rae runs from upstairs and yells out)
I got it Daddy…!

(Opens the front door, both girls kinda screams!)
Oh my JAZZ!!

CANDI RAE!!
Guurl.. Look at you!

Oh no Chica.. Look at you…!
Girl come in!

(Closes the door and they go to chat in the living room)
Oh my god, your hair… I love your hair!!

Ooh Thank you!
So Jazz how's thangs…

Marvelous, I'm feeling great.. Life's great!
Girl, and my Public Relations company, 'ACCIÓN'… business is booming!

I'm so proud of you!
I knew when you two got together, it was magic!

You mean with Rodney?

Yes!

No! … Girl, It's no 'ACTION' with him!
He's done, he didn't know a good thang when he seen it!

Okaay! What happened this time?

You say that like it was my fault...

Guurl... excuse me!..?

Okay it was a little,.. but shit, that don't make me a bad person... Lol

I know it was probably something your lil smart ass said... or did!

Well, a little of both..

What'd you do... or shall I ask... who?

Oooh.. you 'Did Not' go there..!! Hehe

Talk to me Jazlyn! (smile)

Marquise Brimson...!

From the team?? Assistant Coach Brimson??

Yes, and he is a sweetie... Who knew?

Girl... Marquise is 15 years older than you??

Girl... Marquise still got it going on!!
He hittin' that thang like it ain't no tomorrow! ... "Thug style"...! Haha

Lol... Girl U crazy!!...

What about you Candi..?

What about me??

You still growing Cobb Webs on your Coochi since your split with Tyler?

Listen, I'm not growing anything over my stuff... That's just not one of my priorities.

So What is?

It's hard to put into words but, it's a 'Concentrated focus'..!

Girl, you ARE your father's child!

I know, Right!... cool huh!

Girl you'all are so Blessed!

Amen!... Some kids grow up in the family and their parents are referred to,
"Raise 'Em Up" well...
But in my family It's more like, "Coach 'Em Up" well... I Love my Dad..!!

**Okay 'Coach Candi', while in town to see your family and err-thang... we got
some catching up to do, we need to get you outta the house.**

Okayy!!... That Part...
I'm ready to ride Sista.. Where too..?

**Let's go look up some ol friends,
And maybe, someone for a little help with those Cobb Webs..!**

Ooh... You nasty!... Hehe

Thanks for the sandwich Coach... That was good!

Thx! No problem, yeah I feel better now... This has been a hell of a day!

You telling me??

I know Zeph.. I know!!

Man..
Coach, a few hours ago I felt amazing!
I felt as if there was an Angel watching over me... now, where's my Angel..??

Don't feel down, without a doubt it's a crushing situation, but there's always hope!

One thing about me coach is I've lived an extremely good life as an adult,
but as a child, life taught me to be strong,
and that I CAN overcome obstacles that are put in my way...

(and they say simultaneously..)
And this is just another one of them!
And this is just another one of them!... yes Coach, just like you've taught us!

Okay, get your Attny on the phone, I think it's time for you to be planning
your Defense!

True, true..!

(Zeph calls his Attny..)
Listen Zeph, there was another reason why I asked to see you, but it's not
as important as things are right now... we can talk later.

(He hangs up the call and says...)
Hey Coach I'm going to run...
I'm going to head over to see my Attny Karson... he's in the office now.

Ok, that's a good idea.

I told him I was here, he suggest that I keep a distance from you since
you're still apart the team's organization...

Yeah, he's right... It's not a good look...

And to be honest, I don't want you to be apart of this mess either!

Okay Zeph, just know you're in my prayers!

Cool...
Much Luv Coach... I appreciate everything!!

Stay safe Zeph!

Thanks Coach, you too!

TO BE CONTINUED

Coach 'Em Up! S1/3

Candi Rae Hasara (Daughter) = Blue   Jazlyn (Candi's friend) = Orange

---

Coach TJ Hasara (Dad) = Blk   Zephyr (Baller) = Red   Shawna (Attny) = Purple

---

(Candi Rae is riding in the SUV, with Jazlyn as they drive around town)
Dang girl… this is a sweet ride…
I didn't know Bentley makes an SUV model…

They do now! This was the first one, a birthday gift from Marquise! He had it built
by Bentley especially for me!.. So now, they're making them for the public!

Are you serious??

Girl it was all over IG, they even talked about it on TMZ…

But somehow I missed it.. Wow

I'm in Public Relations remember… (smile)
Girl you should get you a Baller too!… speaking of that, who's ride was that at your
dad's house?

Girl that was Zephyr's car!

No Shit? Why didn't you tell me!!

Why, you got a man… your "OG-Thug-Ex Baller-Sugar Daddy"… Lol

Damn, you just had to put it out there like that huh… Lol

He is adorable though…

Who Marquise?

No… Zeph!

Oh THAT'S why you don't want those cobb webs removed... at least for now!

What..??

You tryna catch you a 'Fly Guy' in your web... haha

Jazz you are crazy!!.. But there ARE worst things in life...

I knew your lil freaky butt is up to something... hehe
hey, guess who I ran into the other day...

Who?

Janice and Shawna Smith!

Oh wow... I was thinking about them the other day!
What's up with them?

They said the usual, you know... get up, go to work... back home... repeat cycle!

I haven't seen Shawna in awhile too..

I'm going to text her and say I'm coming by her job to pick her up after work,
she doesn't know you're in town and with me!

Okay... yeah, let's surprise her... hehe

Candi hold the wheel while I text her...

What..??   Oh My God ... JAZZ ... Ooh crap..!

Just hold the wheel and steer... Stop bitchin'
They say it's illegal to text and drive!

Somehow, Me steering this vehicle from the passenger seat is MORE legal to you..??

You're such cry baby Candi... hehe

You're such a psycho Jazz…

But, you still luv me, right?

Crazy chic..! (smile)

Great and I still 'lub' you too!!

**Okay, got a text back from Shawna, she said, "Perfect, to come on by now",
she's "Sitting in on a meeting with a colleague and his client,
but it will be ending soon".**

Excellent! Where does she work?

**She's texting me the address now… Ok, Got it!
Oh that's not far from here.**

Oh yeah..

About 5 minutes

I remember her going off to college, seems like forever…
Did she ever get her degree… What does she do again?

Yes, she's an Attny! Special Counsel for the local YMCA…

Wow, I guess hard work does payoff… that's alright!

Okay, here we are…

Wow, Really Nice office building!

Yea I guess high end clientele…

What? Valet parking too?... Damn!

Niice… That would be for us!… Com'on girl, let's go up!

Yes.. The package came today, heck I got it out of the mailbox myself
**

No, no one has seen it or opened it
**

Well I think it's the right thing to do... it should have been done a long time ago
**

I understand, but it's not about you losing anything, it's about the plain simple truth!
**

It's okay, calm down... we'll get through this as well...
**

No, right now isn't really a good time anyway, there's a lot going on so I'm going to follow my best judgement and hold off on it for now!
**

Ok, Clarissa, I'll be in touch! Calm down and yes, we'll talk later...
**

Ok, sooner...
**

Alright, well, have a Blessed day!... and calm down..

Oh wow, I've never been to an office where the chairs in the lobby were as comfortable as a Lazy boy... sweet!

Hahaha... I know girl.. Wake me up in a few minutes!!

**I know right!! All we need now are some snacks!
We should've stopped for something earlier...**

Well when 'Judge Judy' comes out we can go get something... Lol

You know, for a place like this, they always have refreshments for their clients...

Right... Let's check with the receptionist...

Oh my God.. Candi Rae?...

Shawna!!

Oh wow! What a surprise! Come here girl...

Dang it's good to see you!!
And Oh My God, looks like someone is doing great!!

Uuhum... excuse me...!

Oh, Sorry Jazz... hehe, Come here girl...!

Dang girl, I knew you were doing your thang,
but I didn't know you were doing it like this!

Sometimes it's not about what you know, it's about who you know!
And sometimes when it's a little of both... this is what it looks like! (wink)

Oooh... haha
So what is it you're working on?

Closing a big money deal...?

Oh my god Candi, you shouldn't be here... wish I would have known you were coming!

Why?... Oh, Oh my gosh... Zephyr? Funny seeing you here!

...That's why!!

Candi Rae.. Hi, ... Once Again!

Yep, (a big money deal)... Hi Zephyr, I'm Candi Rae's friend Jazlyn!

Oh gosh Zeph, don't mind her...

Nice meeting you Jazlyn... I've seen you around before, right?

Probably around in the team's organization...

Yeah... that's right... with Coach Brimson, ok!

Small world.. huh!

We were just finishing up here.... For now!

Yes, and we were here to take you away from all of this... For now!

Zephyr, please give your Attny Karson a call in the morning,...
stay off the internet, stay out of the limelight...!!

Yeah, no doubt...

Well we're headed out for a bite to eat, would you like to join us Zeph?

I probably shouldn't be around crowds,
I need to clear my mind, I need to just chill...

I know you're dealing with something that involves my dad as well..
If you don't mind, I'll ride with you.

To where, for what?

To meet up with them, but we need to talk, and this will give us a few minutes to talk.

Zeph, I don't know...

Aww it's cool Shawna, we'll meet up with ya'll, where at?

"De OG's Pound", on West Central Av...

Oooo... I don't know 'bout that... Isn't that Coach Brimson's place...?

Yeah.. It's all good!

It's a nice restaurant/bar, but kind of a higher class.. "Gangsta's Paradise"..!

Yeah, we're just going to be there for a minute to get something to eat

Ok, we'll meet you all there.. But I won't be staying there for long!

You won't have to, we're not going to be long either!!

Okay, let's ride!

Alright Zeph... take care of my girl, AND ask her about those spider webs...

You ass...! (smile)...
Alrighty ladies... See you'all there...!

TO BE CONTINUED

Coach 'Em Up! S1/4

Zephyr (Baller) = Red   Candi Rae Hasara (Daughter) = Blue

Shawna (Attny) = Purple   **Jazlyn (Candi's friend) = Org**   **(Thug) = Grn**

(Candi Rae is in the car riding with Zephyr for a private chat)
Okay Zeph, get to the point, What's going on??
And don't say sports business cause I'm not stupid!
That Attny wasn't a Sports or a Business Attny, he's a Criminal Defense Attny.

Okay Candi, straight up… but if you don't believe me, then what's the point?

Okay then the truth, what's going on, and how is my dad involved?

Your dad is not involved.. It's all on me!
Coach was just informing ME of what's going on…

And what IS going on?

I got kicked off the team…

Yeah right…

No really!

Seriously?... No way!

Yeah, I spent the first half of the day saying 'no way'..!
But trust me.. It's as true as can be!

Oh wow, I'm so sorry to hear that Zeph!

Yeah, thx!

Why?... I mean like… what happened??

A couple of women accused me of two separate physical assaults...

What?... A couple of women?

Yeah... dang girl... this is so embarrassing...

That sounds kinda odd that two women, all of a sudden, would pop up with the same claim...

Exactly, Basically because it's not true!

Zeph with all that you do for the people of the city, helping the homeless, and providing assistance with low income families medical cost...
It's a shame that you'd ever be accused of these charges...

Not only have I lost my job and income, I'm going to start losing my endorsement contracts as well...

And that's a shame too!

It's like a Domino effect, one company drops you, then the others follow suit..

And just like that, they drop you?...
But they don't even have your side of the story yet!

Nope! It's like some unwritten rule, they all do it...
And they don't care what you have to say for yourself!

That's so sad Zeph, we need to get to the bottom of this...

We..?

We,... Us,... Yes .. same people..!

But my Attny suggested that I keep a distance...

Well then here's my number, call or text...

I think they meant distance as in NONE!

You're a big boy Zephyr, you handle your business as you see fit!!

Damn, the lady has spoken... Deal..!
Okay, here it is...

Is this it?

Yeah... "De OG's Pound"...

Nice looking place...

Let's go in and find your girls, then I'm outta here!

Oh there they are,.. just coming in the door...

Try to get their attention, HEYY... oh, they see us...

Hey Ladies..!!

Well it's about time!
I'm not going to ask... but, what took you two so long..? Hehe

Girl please... (smile)

So Zephyr are you headed home now?

Well as a matter of fact Shawna..

Zeph don't you wanna stay for a few, it is kinda cozy

It's nice, but this place isn't for me...

Heyy, watch out… 'CUZ'..!

Who da Hell you talking to… 'BLOOD'..?

I'm just saying brotha!

Just saying What.. you lil punk!

Damn man, what's up wit u.. ain't no need for that..
but you Do Need to back da Hell Up!

Whatcha gunna do!
Beat me like you beat women…??

Zeph, NO.. let it go!!

I know ur lil 'Rollin Deuces' gang boys are all up in here…

You knew where the hell you were, when you walked thru the door!!

I ain't got no beef wit you… at least up in here

So Is that right, well we gotta beef with you!!

ZEPH NO!!

That's right Zeph.. You lil bitches better stick together!

Who you calling a bitch you little asshole!!

Ooh shit.. sorry Ms. Jazz… I didn't know that was you!

You need to get your shit together before Marquise hears about this…

Oh ok… I'm sorry… no disrespect!

It's cool, but you need to 'Get ta Steppin'… Get da hell Up outta here!!

And Zeph, I suggest you do the same!!

Shawna I'm out!!

Oh my God… What was that all about??

These young G's… always flexing… tryna prove a point I guess…

It's nothing Candi, like I was saying, I'm outta here..

Zeph I'm going with you..

Oh No You're Not!!

Com'on Zeph, You've had a horrific day, and this place now gives me the creeps…
It's not my style… Can you drop me off at home please?

ZEPH..??

Either way I'm outta here, you wanna ride Candi Rae… Com'on… Let's ride.

Oh God…

Text me later Candi!

Okay Jazz… Shawna, good seeing you again, we can talk later too!

Okay, drive carefully Zeph, I know you're upset,
and I know what kind of a day you've had… I can't imagine…

Feels like I'm going to explode… I just need to go home and chill..

Yes, go… Tomorrow's another day!

Yeah it'll be better!

Yeah alright, thx, we're out… Later!

Talk to you ladies later!

Later Candi Rae..! (wink)

TO BE CONTINUED

Jazlyn

A SUV Birthday Gift from a Baller

Janice & Shawna

Kaisha

Zephyr (Baller) = Red   Candi Rae Hasara (Coach's Daughter) = Blue

---

(Candi Rae is in the car riding with Zephyr as he drives her home)

Wow I'm at a loss for words!
Zeph what the hell was that all about??

Old stupid shit.. I don't wanna talk about it right now... Uugh!!

Well whatever it is, it's coming back to haunt you...
It's Like everything is working against you... Like that's the agenda!

I'm beginning to get that feeling too!

Like why did that guy in the bar mention you assaulting a female, when the allegations haven't been made public yet?

Damn... You're right!

He knows something...

Thing is, everything that he knows, Marquise knows!
That's how it works...
then that means, it's a good possibility that Jazlyn knows something too!

Whaat?? My friend Jazlyn apart of this? Oh no Zeph, I don't think so...

I'm just saying, she may know something.

Now, I have heard rumors that Coach Brimson had gang ties before,
and even during his playing days...

Yeah, he's actually never stopped!
It's just his player's income and endorsements helped fund his gang activity...

Really..?

**Right now, even though he's a pro ball coach,
he's still an 'OG'...**

An 'OG'.. I've heard that before, what exactly is that?

**An 'Original Gangster'... That means he's been around for awhile,
it also means he's a bad ass!!
Basically he's the Boss.. He calls all of the shots of the gang!...**

NO... WAY!!

He's rumored to be one of the most feared gang leaders around!

OMG... He's been at our house plenty of times having discussions with my dad,
from sports to... religion!

**Well you see how fast that guy straighten up
when he realized that it was Jazlyn that he disrespected!**

And he looked so scared when she mention Marquise's name!!

**I'm tryna tell ya,
They used to say during his playing days,
"He's a very powerful and dangerous man... And he's even worst OFF the field"..!**

Yes, I remember..!!
Remember Marquise's sneaker brand was really popular back in the day
because of that too!

**Yeah, back when he used to hang with Snoop Dogg and 2Pac..
Marquise's 'Thug Style' line of sneakers were dope!...**

Everybody was rockin'em!

Yeah they were really popular in some places, but not on my block.

Do they still make them?

**No, I don't think so... I think they were originally Adidas,
but then Nike took over the contract.**

I don't think they make them anymore either, you don't see or hear
anything about any of his products anymore!

**They phase out certain styles when the player's playing days are over
and aren't as popular anymore ... OR ...
Some new 'Big Time Baller' comes along... (smile)**

Hehe.. Okay Mr. Bigtime Baller!

Hehehe...   Hey, listen Candi Rae... I wanna thank you..!

For what?

For everything... for like, what you just did!

Okayy... but what did I just do?

**This has been a horrible day in many ways,
but it has also had some beautiful moments..
The only few times I've smiled today... are all because of you!!**

Ooooh Zeph, that's so sweet!
Thank You!!

**No, Thank you!
We just left that place and I was mad as hell.. One of the worst days ever!
And now all I can think about is, just how beautiful you are!**

Oh wow Zeph, I bet you say that to all the girls... hehe

Yeah, but it never really works out though... hehe

Well maybe it just wasn't meant to be ... with them!

WHAT?... Candi, look into my eyes.. Tell me you meant that!

You better keep your Eyes on the road... (smile)
and pay attention to where you're going...

(She leans over and kisses him on the cheek)

Okay, so now can I look at you?... (smile)

SMH... (smile)

I'm hungry, I never did get anything to eat...
Can you pull in over there, that looks good!

Yeah, I've eaten there before, it's not bad...

Great, we can have a lil bite before I get home... You don't mind, do you?

Oh noo... It's my pleasure!

Sweet!...Then you get to buy!! (smile)

TO BE CONTINUED

Adam Dumars (ESPN Reporter) = Brn   **Jake Tandy (ESPN News Anchor) = Tan**

Coach TJ Hasara (Dad) = Blk   Clarissa (Coach Hasara's friend) = Pink

---

(On the ESPN Network)
Today on SportsCenter!

Adam Dumars here…
We're live at the Pro Players Conference room standing by to bring you an exclusive
announcement by the team owners!

Adam,… It's Jake Tandy here in the studio…
It's been in the rumor mill that the team is parting ways with one of their more
prolific players in recent history…

Yes Jake, That's what seems to be the word around here as well,
and at this time we can only speculate that it could only be the 3 Time All Pro,
starting wide receiver Zeph Parker…
if so Jake, that would be a tragedy, for the team and the community!
…Oh wait, here comes the team owners now!

(General Manager of the team, Waylan 'Bo' Sheppard steps to the podium)

On behalf of the team owners and myself,
we sadly announce the dismissal of one the most finest athletes that has ever
graced our franchise…
Effective immediately, the player Dexter Lee Parker,
also known as 'Zeph Parker' has been released from the team for violation
of the league's Players' Conduct Policy!
No further comments or questions will be taken at this time… Thank You!

And there you have it Jake… Just as the rumors stated..!
But the big question remains, what could he have done to cause
such a sudden dismissal like that…?

Oh you better believe it Jake... This announcement is rocking the sports world!!

Thanks Adam Dumars for that historic announcement from
The Pro Players Conference room...

And Thank you Zeph Parker for the awesome years of Pro football
entertainment excellence..!
AND...
For the quality work that you've done in the community, and basically, for us all...
We wish you well my friend..!

Now on to other news…. "Tiger Woods" has...

(Back at the Coaches house as he answers the front door)
Clarissa Hi, I thought you were going to wait for my call… Com'on in…

Oh my God TJ, this whole process has been so stressful, my nerves are shot…

Oh I know how you feel, hang in there, everything will be alright..
Can I get you something to drink?

No… I'm okay, thank you…!

What ever the truth is, it needs to be told

I sure hope You're right.

I sure hope We're right!
You know what that'll mean… for me, for you, and for… our SON!

I know how much you have always wanted to call him your son…

And the times that you've spent together,
I know every moment of it has touched your heart.

Yes, it's an awesome feeling..! Some guys are so lucky!

But, It's not the same unless you truly know,
as the old saying goes,... "Momma's baby... Poppa's maybe"...

Well, all you have to do is open that package from D&A Diagnostics,
and read the results to know!

Yeah I know, but I just thought that It would be a special moment,
and I wanted to wait for the right time, BUT today has been crazy..!

How's that??

(Just then the coach's cellphone rings)
See…. Just like that… Like I said, it's been a crazy day!
Excuse me Clarissa, I need to take this call…

Hello…!
**

Adam Dumars, how are you…?
Let me guess… you want a comment from me!
**

Because I've been doing this for a long time too, that's how I know!
**

And Yes, so you know very well, the team's standpoint of no comments extends to me as well…
**

No.. I'm not sure, I wasn't in any meetings to know
**

Well Adam, honestly, if you hear anything, can you please let ME know!
**

Yes I do care… for all of them…!
They're all fine talented young men, my heart goes out to Zephyr…
I just hope and pray for the best, for him!
**

That's great, I'll be in touch,
Thanks a lot Adam,… take care!

That was an ESPN reporter, Adam.

You're not going to believe this…

There was just a live announcement by the team's ownership on ESPN that 'Zephyr'… has been released from the team!!

Yes, today is April 1st... That's a true fact..!
And so is the fact that, 'Zeph Parker' is no longer on the team..!!

Yes… I am very serious…!!

Your… Son/Our… Son… has been released from the team…!!

TO BE CONTINUED

Shawna (Attny) = Purple   Jazlyn (Marquise's girlfriend) = Org

---

Asst. Coach Marquise Brimson (Ex Baller, OG) = Dk Grn

(Back at the "De OG's Pound"...)
So where's Marquise, I'm surprised he's not here in the club

Checking my text now... I got a text from him not long ago, he said he's on his way, my guess is he'll be here soon...

Why is that?

I'm sure he's heard about that lil thing with Zephyr by now.

Yeah, I'm sure

An anyway, he knows his baby is in here!!

Yess.. and she can't wait to see him!

He just does something to me... girl I can't put it into words..!

I know what you mean, and I think your body language says it all...

It shows huh... (smile)

Just a little..!

(Marquise Brimson arrives at their table)
My, My, My,... How's my favorite ladies!
Hey Baby!.. *(kisses Jazlyn)*
Shawna!.. *(kisses Shawna)*

Look at you Marquise!.. you're looking happy... How are you Baby?

A lil birdie sang me a sweet song tonight...

That sounds sweet, but what's going on?

One of the lil soldiers told me that Zeph was in the place earlier...

Oh yeah he was, for about five or ten minutes...

Un huh... told me he was causing some problems and had to be put in check.

It was minor, it was really nothing.

Well the beauty is in the eye of the beholder!

What'd ya mean?

Well that lil incident was caught on video!

What?... By who?

One of the customers got cellphone footage of a lil pushing and shoving...

Oh really?

Yeah, a customer recognized Zeph,
pulled out their phone and started videoing him...
Then one of my people happen to be walking by and Zeph bumped into him
for no reason, and started an incident!

Oh my gosh... That's not quite how it happened...

Wait... But That's PERFECT..!

EXACTLY, and the best part is,
it ties everything together into one nice little package.

How's that?

That video has been, as we say, 'Retouched'...
Then uploaded onto the internet... It's on Fb, IG and most social media platforms...

Great!
I'll have my IT people get to work on it immediately,
we'll blow it up and make it go viral...

Did the team release Zeph this evening?

Yes!... ESPN announced it not long ago,
and tomorrow the rest of the plan will come into full play!

Excellent, tomorrow the allegations will be made public..

Shawna are the Victims ready?

Oh yes, they are so distraught..!

Niice!

Their Attny Dallas, she's on top of every aspect and has everything in place,
there'll be no links back to us at all...

What about Zeph's Attny?

Karson... Nicc guy! He's an extremely sharp guy too,
graduated at the top of his class from Law school...
BUT, a few promises here and there... a nice deposit into his account,
and he was like putty in my hands... twice!

Damn Shawna you're good!

Better believe it, that's why you pay me the big bucks!...
And I'm just getting started..

My Public Relations company has 'Phase Two' all ready to implement!
"Lights, Cameras… Acción"..!

Cool… Let's do it!
Oh yeah, one more thang, who was the chic with Zeph tonight?

Oh crap.. That's right, that was Candi Rae… Coach Hasara's daughter!

Who?.. I thought his daughter name is Kaisha?

Everyone always says that… yes, but there's two other daughters that lives in the Caribbean with their mother, and that was his middle daughter!

Oh really!!... And she's dating Zeph??

NO Marquise!!… Don't even think about it..!!
That's my girl, and she's off limits..

Oooh look at you.. Getting all powerful and shit!
Okay, well she's off limits…

Good…

Oh, but one thang though…

What's that?

If she becomes a problem… It's your ass that has to pay!
And I'm glad 'YOU' understand that in advance!

And with that being said, Com'on everybody,
let's get out of here…

TO BE CONTINUED

Zeph Parker (Baller) = Red   Candi Rae Hasara (Daughter) = Blue

---

(Back at the restaurant where Zephyr and Candi Rae are having dinner)
Zeph, those people over there are staring at you.

I think they are staring at you…
Oh girl, you and your smile… and your hair… simply gorgeous!

Thank you! My younger sister NaKira created this hair style… This is one of her, 'Signature Styles'..!

Very niice..! I like that lil touch of violet!
Maybe she can do something with my dreads… It's getting too hot for this!

Hehe… I'll see, but you are going to have to take a long trip to get it done!

From what I understand, I have the time!

Yeah, that's right

I am going to call my agent Dru later,
I need him to start getting geared up for negotiations…

Wow, you make it all seem so… routine!

It is, that's how this league is…
nothings permanent… only change!

That's why they call it the… (NFL)… 'Not-For-Long'…!

Hehe.. Yeah, That's an old one…

Yeah, I know… But still very true!

Excuse me Candi Rae….

Hello, Yes..!
**

Dru, man you must have heard me thinking about you!
**

Yeah, we knew it was coming so no real shocker, but just the way it all came down!
**

Yeah, we know it's all BS, but how can we move forward, without all of this NOT effecting negotiations?
**

I know, at this point negations aren't the problem, no team wants to even talk until all of the dust has settled…
**

Of course I'm a fighter! I think I will get a private investigator!
**

Well talk to him, fly him in… whatever… don't worry about the cost and fees… just have him to get started immediately!
**

Excellent, you da man Dru!
Hit me up if you need me…. Later!

Excuse me for over hearing your conversation… But maybe you can have that P.I. start snooping around Coach Brimson's place. At lease it's a starting point.

**Well, the P.I. isn't in town yet, I'll relay the message..
but then let the P.I. follow his own leads…**

I think we we're on to something…

**Yeah, but there may be far more to it than what we can see…
So meanwhile, I guess I'm to keep a low profile!**

You deserve it, with what you've been through, a break will do you good!

Yeah, I'm just ready to get home and relax... I can hear my hot tub calling my name!

Is it whispering your name, or calling you loudly? (Hehe)

Softly, she's saying, Zepphhh... Oh Zepprey..!! Lol

Lol... Oh Yeah... so how does she sound when she's mad??

Are you kidding, I'm not going to get her mad at me!! Oh no... Lol

Well can I meet her?

Huh.. YES!!

No, I better not... never mind...

Wait Candi... I would really like...
Well, I should say, It would be my honor to show you around my place!

Well, maybe I spoke too soon...

There's no better time than the present...
Sometimes it's nice to live in the now!

No doubt, I have a question for you...

What's that?

So if your hot tub can call your name... does she sing to you too? (smile)

Haha.. You should Com'on over and check her out...
she sounds like Patti La Belle!

Hehehe... Very tempting.. But.. I'm going to head home, maybe next time!

It's my first day in town and I haven't spent any time with my dad since I've been here.

Hold on... Excuse me Candi...

Go ahead, I know it's important.

Thank you...
It's a reporter from ESPN...

Yes... Hello!
**

Yeah, thanks... you're welcome!
**

No Adam, I don't have any comments at this time.
**

What do you want me to say...
**

I'm not sure why... WAIT... This is off the record correct?
**

I'm serious man, this is off the record right?
**

Okay, if NOT...
**

Ok Adam... you know this is a setup right!
**

I'm not sure, off the record right... Brimson know something!
**

Yeah Coach Brimson...
**

I don't know, but it's something to do with him...
**

Great! Hey my agent has a friend who's coming into town for a little 'I SPY' work!
I'm going to have them contact you!
**

Cool.. I'll be in touch! ... Later..

Sorry about that Candi..

No worries... I understand...
Are you about ready to go Zeph?

Sure, let me take care of this bill, and we're out...
This at least, was a really nice evening compared to earlier today.

I know this has been a long day for you as well...

Yeah, but a very interesting day to say the least!
And dinner was good... Thank you!

Oh yes, it was good, and it's no problem, it's my pleasure..
Okay, I'm all set... Are you Ready?..

Yes..

Alright, let's go..!

TO BE CONTINUED

__________________ *Cast of Players* __________________

Coach Hasara: Black
Head Coach of the Professional Football Team

Zephyr: Red
Footballer, Wide Receiver on Hasara's team

Candi Rae Hasara: Blue
Daughter of Coach Hasara

Jazlyn: Orange
Friend of Candi Rae, Girlfriend of Marquise B.

Shawna: Purple
Old friend of Candi Rae and Jazlyn

Marquise Brimson: Dk. Grn
Asst. Coach of Hasara, Ex-footballer, Boyfriend of Jazlyn

Clarissa: Pink
Old friend of Coach Hasara

Adam Dumars: Dk. Brn
ESPN News Reporter

Grace Seavers: Lt. Blue
Private Investigator

Half Time

Candi Rae

Head Coach TJ Hasara

Zephyr

Clarissa

P.63

Benjamin (Nike Exec.) = Dk Brn   **Maxwell (Nike Product CEO) = Lt Brn**

Coach TJ Hasara (Dad) = Blk   Clarissa Parker (Coach's Ex-Lover) = Pink

---

Zephyr Parker (Baller) = Red   Candi Rae Hasara (Daughter) = Blue

---

(At the Nike US Headquarters)

Maxwell, can you come to my office when you have the complete info…

Got it, I'm on my way sir!

Okay, have a seat… What all do you have?

Well yes sir the team did release the player, no certain facts on what, how and reasons why… yet sir!

These things are always covered up in the beginning.
Have your people dig deep…

You just don't toss out your star player for minor infractions!

Our people are on it sir!
What about the product release planned for next week of the new 'Zephyr Fire' line?

As much as I'd like to see it happen, as of now we're temporarily pulling the plug!
Everything's.. on hold until further notice!

What about the ads that are already in place and running..?

Temporarily pull everything, I hate seeing this kind of thing happen,
But, I don't want any backlash from any directions!

Yes sir, especially since we're still not sure what all we're facing…

As a matter of fact, get his agent Dru on the phone,
let's see if he'll have a word or two with us...

We've tried for awhile now sir, so far still no reply..

You know how it goes, keep trying... but soon, he'll be calling us!

No doubt.. Just a matter of time! We'll keep at it...

(Back at the coach's house)
Thanks for the drink TJ, now I need it.

I think I'll have one too!

Why, why did all of a sudden the team release my son?

The reason they gave was conduct policy violations...

What does that mean?

Well I know that Zephyr went to see his Attny to get everything under control,
it's just that it may take a little time first..

We're all having an emotional day...

You can say that again.. Sometimes, things can get you down,
but you have to have hope and pray for strength...

It's never really easy, I guess it's what you make it!

True,.. have you ever just dreamed of a perfect world?

Sometimes I can picture one.. Then I wake up!

Hehe I hear ya... I think we do have those 'perfect moment' thoughs, probably
so that we can remember them when we're so deep into our own situations.

Yes, I like to think back sometimes to my college years.

Oh yeah, why's that?

Well it was kinda scary, kinda exciting... But I feel I really came into my own then...
I found the real me!

I see, I think that happened for me in my 30's...
Around the age of 33... I finally felt grown up then!

Me Too!!

Funny, how we can look back on that, like it was yesterday!
I was forty pounds less.. Head full of hair!

Zephyr dreadlocks reminds me of the time we met in Barbados...

Oh my gosh, sorry about that... Too much Rum Punch! (hehe)

Haha... That was an awesome night.. I enjoyed every minute!
That's all I'm gonna say..! (smile)

Oh my, lady you looked fantastic!

Now that was the rum punch talking... Lol

No, but it's true, the rum couldn't control that part!

Yeah right...

I didn't have anything to do with the part where someone put on that Marvin Gaye
album... Oooh Girl..!

Haha.. I bet you didn't

Well actually, I did kinda slip the DJ a twenty...!

WHAT? All these years I wondered...

And we danced all night! (smile)
Come here, let me hold you... You in my arms always felt so right!

Funny, this is where I felt I should be...

Clarissa, you should've been...
We all make mistakes, and I've definitely made my share...

Oh it's okay TJ, that's water under the bridge...
we can only live for today, and not even for tomorrow!

So true!...

(As they embraces and kiss)
Clarissa... baby, mmm..

This does feels so, so right.. TJ

Do you wanna...?

I'm with you baby..

Let's go upstairs!

Mmm.. Let's go...!

(Zephyr and Candi Rae arrive into the circular driveway of the coach's house)
Mmm.. Thanks for everything Zeph, I appreciate the ride, the dinner... the conversation...
Even under these circumstances,
this was a really good day!

**Yeah.. I'm really happy I've had a chance to meet you,
and get to spend this afternoon and evening with you as well..**

Yeah, actually made this day incredibly interesting, Thanks!

And you've brighten mine, thank you!
Looks like the coach has company... my mom has a car like that.

Yeah, he's a popular guy on any given day, and just so happens,
as a Head Coach who's just lost one of his starting star players today,
I'm sure there has been many visits and calls...

True! Well, all we can do is hope all of this gets sorted out soon...

I'm sure the reporter and the private investigator will get to the truth..

Right, I hope they can get to the bottom of this soon..
It's one thing to create your own problems, but it is really devastating when it's a plot
against you!

Hang in there Zeph, you have the truth on your side, and everyone's praying for the truth
to be known!

Thanks, that's alright Candi.. Com'on, let me walk you to the door...

Ok.. You know what, come on inside Zeph, there's something I wanna give you...

Ooh really?

It's not what you think.. silly

Oh no I wasn't...

(they go inside into the living rm)
See, It's a good luck charm!!

Oh nice..

I seen it in the airport and thought it was so cute...
I want you to have it!

Oh Yeah! Thank you… But why?

Cause right now, you need this more than I do… and I wish you all the luck in the world!

Oh my gosh Candi Rae, girl, wow… you are so sweet… Come here…

*(As they embraces and kiss, Coach Hasara walks down the stairs, partially naked…
And everyone is caught completely off guard..!!)*

OH MY GOD..! "ZEPHYR"..!!

"COACH"..!!

"DADDY"..!!

"CANDI"..!!

(And now Clarissa is standing at the top of the stairs, and says:)

"ZEPHYR"..!!

…MOMMA..??
Wait a minute, … WTF??

TO BE CONTINUED

Coach 'Em Up! S1/10

Adam Dumars (ESPN Reporter) = Brn   Grace Seavers (Private Inv.) = Lt Blu

---

Marquise Brimson (Ex Baller, OG) = Dk Grn   Shawna (Attny) = Purple

---

Jazlyn (Marquise's girlfriend) = Org

(Phone call...)
Hello, this is Adam...

Adam, Hi.. Grace Seavers, Private Investigator!!

Yes... Hi

I was hired to investigate this case on behalf of Dexter Lee Parker!

Yes, He informed me that you would be contacting me... How can I help you?

*I'll be arriving in town tomorrow morning, and I wanna hit the ground running,
my reputation is that of being very thorough, and meticulous...*

I hear ya, so what is it I can do for you..?

*Two things, Keep an ear out for anything to do with Assistant Coach Brimson, I know you
have the insider's ear by him being an ex-ball player!*

Yes, definitely, I'm on it!

Also there's chatter going around the internet about a video...

A Video, what video?

*My people have just started to look into it and so far,
it appears to be trending mainly because the view count is being inflated artificially...*

Why is that? And what's on the video?

I'm not sure, that was intel from a bloggers site, but someone is trying
to drive that video into going viral...

Really... S.O.B.!
And if it has anything to do with Zephyr, I see where you're going with this...
Gotta admit, there's some strange things happening...

Yeah, that's why I need you to do this second part...

What's that?

Pick me up from the airport in the morning,
by then I think that video will have actually taken on a life of it's own,
and then goes viral for sure...

Wow...

Yeah, then our work will be cut out for us!

Okay, well text me the details of your flight,
get some sleep,
and I'll see you in the morning... Grace!

Thanks, will do... But, ... I don't sleep!!

(Marquise gives Shawna a call)
Hey um Shawna... You home?

Yeah, I had Jazlyn to just drop me off at home...

Oh ok, that's right, you left your car at the office today.

Yeah, I'll have my girlfriend Janice drop me off at the office in the morning...
I'll get it then... so, 'What're u doin'...??

... I'm just driving around, doing a little thinking...

This whole plan, I mean, It's almost... genius!
Once the dust settles, I'll own the property that old YMCA is sitting on...
And tear that old ass building down...

He'll never get his money out of it... just letting the kids run around
and play there...

You know it's true... that location is a cash cow for my businesses,
I need that spot...
Hey, and I'm doing it the legal way!

We used to just put the gun barrel to some MF's head...
give 'em a ink pen and say, sign right here...
No negotiations were necessary.. at least not on my part...!

I know right... And you don't see the beauty in that?

Baby, that's called growth!! Anyway.. I'm Just bullshittin'...
but on the real, a lot of this was payback to Zeph, from way back in the day.

I know, I'm the one who thought of a few ideas, But You're the sadistic one who came up with the rest of that shit...

I know baby, we conceive, create, and execute brilliantly together!!

Yeah, you talking bout that sexy part.. Right?

Haha... that time I was actually talking about the plan...
but as you can tell,.. yes.. I am turned on!!

Is there a time when you're not?

Who's keeping track... but you know me..

I'm not too far away, I'll swing by..

Okay mmm... that sounds good,
Janice and I are about to jump into the shower... Hurry up, ...
I don't want you to miss out!

Girl... I like the way you think... I'm on my way..!

(And Marquise's girl Jazlyn, is on a call herself...)

Rodney, heyy baby.. so, 'What're u doin'...??

TO BE CONTINUED

Coach 'Em Up! S1/11

Coach TJ Hasara (Dad) = Blk   Clarissa Parker (Coach's Ex-Lover) = Pink

---

Candi Rae Hasara (Daughter) = Blu   **Zephyr Parker (Baller) = Red**

Benjamin (Nike Exec.) = Dk Brn   **Maxwell (Nike Product CEO) = Lt Brn**

(At the Coach's house…)

Oh My God Daddy… why are you Yelling…??
Why are you so Shocked and Upset??

Candi, baby… Ugh… You Don't Understand!
HOW IN DA HELL…?

**What are you talking about Coach, we didn't Cross the Line,
It was just a little kissing…**

OH MY GOD..!
That WAS crossing the Line!

Calm down TJ… You've got to explain..

HOW CAN I CALM DOWN…?

Yes please explain… There seems to be more going on here than just, 'US'…!

RIGHT..! Momma… What are you doing here… and Naked??

I'm not naked.. But I AM very embarrassed… Oh I gotta get dressed…

Daddy I think you should too..

Oh gosh, Yeah… Don't you two go anywhere.. Let me put on something,
we'll be back down in a minute!

Oh my... Who knew the night would be like this...

Now I can say, this has truly been The Most Screwed Up day ever!...
Man... What else could go wrong..?

Baby never, ever, ask that question...

Maxwell, what do you have?

Apparently there's a video of the player Zeph Parker in a known street gang bar/hangout...
He appears to be a trouble maker, even in that tough environment, he's doing some pushing and shoving of some of the customers!!

Wow, so are there any other reports of misconduct?

Not that we have so far, but we'll stay on it...
But one more thing..

What's that?

Head Coach Hasara's daughter was in the bar with the player...

Are the player and the Coach's daughter dating?

Not sure, but this thing could possibly involve the coach as well...

Yeah, he's been very quiet, out of the limelight...

Maybe there IS something there too...?

Have you heard from his agent Dru yet?

No.. Still no word!

It's still early... when that video is available from being downloaded, let me know...

Zeph's agent will be crawling back to talk to us soon!!

Yeah, then he'll see who actually controls things!!

(Back At the Coach's house...)

Daddy we have so many questions..

I know, and the answers are basically stories from our lives...

How's that?

Yeah, I don't get it..

Well, ok everybody, let's all have a seat.

Talk about how we first met...

Yeah, how did you two meet? And when?

Many years ago, Clarissa and I met in Barbados on Spring Break!

It was awhile ago, but it seems like yesterday...

We instantly hit if off, and spent a Fabulous week together and then after that..

We went separate ways, back to our lives but, we kept in touch!

Yes, we had separate lives me as a student athlete, and Clarissa as a music major studying Classical Piano!

We were to meet up again the following year, same location..

But Clarissa didn't show up... and no word from her...
and that spring is when I met, your mother Candi...!

So Ms. Parker, excuse me for asking, but why didn't you show up?

Oh don't you know... it was obvious, I had just had a new born...
My little bundle of joy... Dexter!

And I didn't know the reasons, I didn't have a clue...

No, you were busy being that great sports guy.. That was your calling, I made sure our baby was very well taken care of..!

SO HOLD UP...!!!
Are you two saying that... Coach I'm your SON..?? You're my Father??

WHATT...??

(And Zeph and Candi Rae says simultaneously..)
Are you Freakin Kiddin Me?? ... (smh)
Are you Freakin Kiddin Me?? ... OH WOW...!!

No that's the truth in how it all happened...
and so where we stand today is...
We're in the process of learning the truth of your paternity.

When will you find out?

Right now, if you all are interested, I've received the DNA test results back, but haven't opened the envelope yet!

Wait, those results will change a few things immediately for sure...

I guess we all should stop to think what's all involved with learning the results...

Regardless, it still has to be known... the truth IS STILL the truth!

All I can say is, What a Day..!!

No, I believe the time to learn the truth is far overdue!
Clarissa can you pass me that envelope please… Thank you!

Here you go… This is sorta exciting and scary!!

No Momma, this is so unreal…

Okay, let's see… what does it say Daddy?

Let's see… It says…

"The results as pertaining to:

Timothy Juan Hasara, as to the parent of one, Dexter Lee Parker…

Mr. Hasara, You ARE… (NOT) the Father"

TO BE CONTINUED

Adam Dumars (ESPN reporter) = Brn   Grace Seavers (Private Inv.) = Lt Blu

---

Zephyr (Baller) = Red   Coach TJ Hasara (Dad) = Blk   Shawna (Attny) = Purple

---

Marquise Brimson (OG) = Dk Grn   Jazlyn (Marquise's Girlfriend) = Org

---

(At the airport baggage claim area)
Hi…. Are you Grace? … Grace Seavers..?

Yes, and you must be Adam… I recognize you from tv, Good morning!

Yes, Good morning, nice to meet you!
Wow… You told me that you were thorough and meticulous,
but you forgot to mention how gorgeous you are!

What a nice way to be greeted into town! (smile)

Thanks, how was your flight?

Informative… I have some news on that video!

Oh yeah, and while you were in flight,
I have more news from on the ground…

What now?

A couple of women and their Attny just brought forward formal complaints
against Zephyr for physical assaults.

Oh really? But how did he assault two women at the same time?

Allegedly, there were two separate incidents…

So he has a pattern of this type of behavior?

Never heard of anything before but I'm sure at his level of being a pro ball player, and celebrity spokesperson, he's become a target of all types of scams...

But on the other hand if the allegations are true...
Let justice be served!

Well, the truth is what we'll find, justice is what everyone deserves...

Oh Yeah.. Tell me about the video...

Just as I thought, It has taken off... it's now in the category of being viral.

What's on it?

Our beloved football star, in a bar... starting some mess!
It was just a little trash talking but it seems like there's a pattern building.

But here's the kicker.. Coach Hasara's daughter was with him..!

You're kidding right? ... I thought Kaisha lives in DC..?

Not sure, that's all I know...

Wow... So where do we start?

Where else... Let's go visit the good ol' coach!!

Why is that... The coach is a very gentle and docile guy!

It's a good starting point, maybe he wanted him off the team for reasons to do with his daughter... Do you have kids Adam?

Yes, two girls... They live with their mother.

And what wouldn't you do to protect them...?

Mmm ... I Gotcha ... Let's go see the coach!

Dru, hey man... Good morning..
**

No, I'm just waking up, what's going on?
**

Yeah, the allegations... I knew that was coming...
**

What video?
**

WHAT?? ... Get the hell outta here!!
**

Oh damn, but that was just yesterday, and it's already gone viral?
**

Yeah, I know how it works, you can't control what people post online.
**

What other part...
**

OoH SHIT..!!
 ...No, no that's coach's other daughter... that's my um, ... that's Candi Rae!
**

What? .. Oh my god, No!
Coach doesn't have anything to do with any of this !!
**

I can imagine how it must look...
**

With all of this going on, there's something else...?
**

OH DAMN..!!!
I completely forgot about the Nike new product line release next week!!
**

Oh no... You haven't contacted them yet?
**

Yeah, I can Imagine everything's being put on hold...
**

Well, do what you can, but I understand how it goes...
Hit me up when you know something!
 .. Later..

Ladies.. Great morning!!

Hey Marquise, you're up early... and I'm sure I know why

How'd you sleep baby?

Like a baby..!
Shawna I seen the news this morning, everything looked great!

It all went just as planned! The victims were convincing!

Great, great press conference.

Yeah, I was feeling sorry for them... for a second!

And from what I can see, our lil friends' video may be up for an Oscar! .. Lol

Jazz, your people definitely has the skills..!

It's that Midas touch baby.. Everything we touch, turns to Gold!

Well all of this shit has become, Golden!!

Let's all get together later... I need to unwind with a drink by the hot tub...

I have some serious business to take care of later today, we'll see.

About what time?

I can't really say...

Around what area of town... never mind, but if you're in my area, say hi...

I'm thinking today is going to be a great day as well..!!

Well It has started out that way!
 Alright, Later...

Okay Grace, how are you going to go about asking the coach if he has anything to do with Zephyr's demise?

Haha... Well I'm actually going to toss one question out at him, the rest of the conversation will be played from that answer.

I see, he is a very 'talk-ative' person.

Great, sometimes we in law enforcement basically let the people incriminate themselves...

It's kinda like fishing..?

It's called, good police work! ... Com'on let's go talk to the coach.

Good morning, Hi Coach Hasara... I'm Grace Seavers, Private Investigator! And this is Adam...

I know his face... (smile)
Hi Grace... Nice to meet you! ... Grace, Adam ...Com'on in!

Wow, really nice home sir!

Thank you, So what is it I can do for you this morning?

As you know Coach were investigating the issues with Zephyr...

Yes, and I was brought in to investigate on behalf of Mr. Parker

Okay, so how can I help?

Can you tell me about your relationship with Mr. Parker?

Wow, you start out punching a sore spot.

Oh it's just some personal stuff we've been dealing with..

Yes… but what does this have to do with anything?

Hey don't be playing that cop stuff with me,
you need to be out there getting to the bottom of this mess..

What are you looking at Adam?

Nothing coach… but um, you just reminded me of Zephyr…

What??

You see, there's a video floating around the internet with Zephyr,
in a bar… causing some ruckus..

And what does that have to do with me?

It's reported, that female is your daughter!

Candi Rae?

Who?? … Who's Candi Rae?

That's my daughter…

I thought your daughter's name is Kaisha?

Kaisha's my oldest daughter…

Where's she?

Who?… Kaisha?

Nooo…! Candi Rae..?

Oooh, She's upstairs..!

Can we speak to her?

She had a long emotional day yesterday, and she's sleeping in this morning…
Maybe I can have her to give you a call later…

Okay coach thanks, here's my card… Oh and one more thing…

What's that?

Did you happen to see the press conference this morning?

No I missed it… What was it on?

Ya' boy, Zeph..! You should give him a call…
We'll be in touch Coach!

Talk to you later Coach…

Okay, where to now Grace?

I recv'd information from my team that they did a trace on that video's traffic

Oh yeah… What did they come up with?

They found that the numbers that were driving that video into going viral were originating from overseas servers...

And why from overseas?

Probably trying to conceal their identity by being non-traceable... and it's illegal..

Wow, so now what?

I said trying to be... we were still able to trace the computer server's IP address..!!

Nice!

It appears that all of the servers had recv'd command communication from a main controller computer, and that main computer is local, right here in town!

You don't say... So where's that location?

They traced it to a street address Downtown, near Jackson St...
It's called,.... "Acción Public Relations"...

Well let's go have a little chat, let's see how well they relate to us, .. the public...!

TO BE CONTINUED

Grace

Marquise

Adam

Hustle Man

Coach 'Em Up! S1/13

Adam Dumars (ESPN reporter) = Brn   Grace Seavers (Private Inv.) = Lt Blu

---

Corina (P.R. Assistant) = Lt Grn   Jazlyn (friend) = Org   **Marquise B. (OG) = Dk Grn**

(Sitting in the parked car...)
Okay Grace, If they did inflate the viewer counts to make that video go viral,
they aren't going to just tell us they did it...

So what's the strategy?

Mmm, let's do a little acting,... Let's pretend to be potential clients,
I'll be Danica... You'll be... Mr. Albright! ...
Just follow my lead!

Ok Cool... I got this!

(They arrive at the front office of Acción PR)
Hi.. I'm Danica Jones.. Video/Film Producer!

Oh Hi Ms. Jones... We've heard so much about you!... Awesome work!

Oh really.. Well um, thank you! But call me Danica...

Well what can I do for you, Danica..

My client here, 'Mr. Albright' will be featured in a film documentary and we wanna
increase the volume of viewers and traffic to his videos and website!

Oh yes, that is one of our many services...

Great!

We can start with print ads and tv spots and your traffic will increase at a
managed rate!! How's that sound...?

Really, this is the big leagues… this is a fast paced world,
hell we could be dead and gone by the time all of that happens…

Well for our specialty clients on a time frame, we have an Urgency Promotion!…

What's that?

Well we can promote your video online overseas…
the Europeans love our stuff…

And what would that do for us?

Well we could probably increase your viewer numbers almost over night!!

(I guess they do love us in the EU…)

So is it a proven thing or are you just hoping that will work?

Oh it's very effective, proven successfully time and time again!

Oh okay, just between us… give me an example,… a lil hint..

Well… you didn't hear it from me, but…
There's a Pro Football star's video that was just boosted,
check YouTube, you'll know which one…

Very Nice… Is that the one with Candi Rae and Zephyr??

Who??… Who's Candi Rae?
All I know is,… it's Zephyr..!

Great, So how Do We get started as clients?

You'll need to speak to Ms. Summers to get all of your info and plans started…
But, she's running a little late today…

And Who is she?

Jazlyn Summers, oh she's the accounts manager, And she's also the owner…
Her man is ex footballer, Marquise Brimson..!

Oh Really..!!
I see… so I guess everything goes through her?

Yes!…

…and you are?

Oh excuse me, I'm her assistant, Corina Lozano!

Well thank you Corina, you have been so so helpful..!

Oh, aren't you going to wait for Ms. Summers?

No, but you can give her my card, thx … I will be in touch!

I'm looking at this card, but I don't get it… Who's Grace Seavers?
Private Investigator…??

Just relay the message… Thanks Corina.

(As Grace and Adam sit in the car to leave the office)

Oh my god she was a wealth of information!

Yeah, right!!

So we're right on the money when it comes to following the trail..

So with that info, where to now?

Well there's that name of Coach Brimson again…
He may be the common denominator in this whole equation…

During football season he never holds interviews, and he's so hard core, how can you get any information from him?

Guys like him you don't get info from, you have to give them some info, then watch them run with it...

And what do you give him?

It's what we just gave him... Notice!!

I don't get it..

The word will get back to him that we are hot on the trail...

And what good will that do?

He'll know there's flaws in his plan,
and so now he'll have to make adjustments...

And what do we get in return?

...Hopefully, not killed..!

Yes, she was asking questions about the business, and what we could do for her...
**

She wanted to know about the Urgency promotions...
**

She also wanted to know about Zephyr's video...
And who's Candi Rae, she said she was in the video too...?
**

No I didn't tell her ANYTHING... I told her she had to speak to you!
**

Okay, I'll see you when you get in...

ARE YOU KIDDING ME??... IT'S BEEN LESS THAN 24 HOURS AND I ALREADY HAVE A PRIVATE INVESTORGATOR SNOOPING AROUND MY PLACE!!

Chill girl, don't get all flustered...

WHAT?? ... IM NOT USED TO ALL THIS "GANSTER LIFE" STUFF...
I CAN'T LIVE MY LIFE "HAPPILY" IN PRISON...

We got this under control, don't worry bout nothing..

Oh yeah Marquise... So how does she know of Candi Rae's name?
What did you do Marquise??

What are you talking about, I didn't give nobody no names...

You were the only one that had a interest in Candi Rae!

You need to back up baby girl... Don't mess with me about that chic!

You brought her into all of this, I told you she was off limits!!

Who the hell you think you're talking to Jazz, I CAN MAKE YOUR ASS GO AWAY
FOREVER!! ... DON'T FUCK WITH ME!!

Oh you're gonna THREATEN ME MARQUISE...??

JUST DON'T CROSS THE LINE WITH ME JAZZ ... I'M NOT GONNA TELL YOU ANYMORE ...
THAT'S MY WORD!!

TO BE CONTINUED

Coach 'Em Up! S1/14

Marquise B. (OG) = Dk Grn   Jazlyn S. (friend) = Org   Shawna (Attny) = Purple

---

(Marquise on a phone call to one of his gang's Lieutenants…)
Hey Yo Trey… Yo listen… I got something I need you to go do…
****

No no, it's not that thang yet.. That's later
****

I have some loose ends that need taken care of…
****

An afterwards, I need you to do a car repo…
****

Man take some people with you,
I need you to go get my Mu-fuckin car back from Jazz..
****

She should be at her office all day…
****

I know she's not going to go along with it…
****

Well if you have to, put a couple of shells in her head…
****

HELL YEAH IM SERIOUS!!
****

Hey and um Trey…
Don't get no blood and shit in my new car!!

(Back at Jazlyn's Public Relations office..)
Shawna..?? .. What are you doing here?

Jazz listen, you're in danger!
We don't have a lot of time… I'll explain on the way…!

What are you talking about? Oh the way to where?

We need to get you out of this office…

We're going to a very private, well I should say, a secret location!

Did Marquise put you up to doing something?

No, but Jazz... We need to get you out of here ASAP!

WHAT? And how would you know??

Jazlyn... I'm an undercover agent..

YOU'RE A COP..??

 Im actually a Special Agent for Alcohol Tobacco and Firearms!!

What the Hell??... You're an ATF AGENT?

Yes!!... and Marquise has been under surveillance by a joint task force
of the FBI, DEA and ATF..!

OMG, So what's going on, why are you here??

Marquise... Well, he wants you dead...
And he's sending some people over here soon!

Oh my God... There's Some Guys Outside.. They're Outside Already...!!

Those guys are with me to help extract you out of here... so we gotta go, NOW!

Oh my God...!

Oh my God is right, you'll be alright, just follow my directions, and let's go..!!

**Shawna... this is crazy! How long have you been an agent, how long have you been
undercover??**

Since before you met Marquise he's been under surveillance...
You know his dealings, you know his way of life!

So you said he's coming after Me?

Yes, he now thinks that you're a loose end that threatens his operation.

Oh God..! How did all this start?

From what we can tell, Marquise has plans for his gang to branch out
and take over 3 or 4 major cities in this area of the state.

I knew that there's a big situation going on... but that's bout it...

Com'on Jazz... are you forgetting who you're talking to!!

No seriously Shawna, I don't know of any take over plans..

Well for him to complete the takeover, his people needed some heavy fire power...
That buy for military grade weapons from some international arms dealers is due
to go down tonight... And we can't let those weapons hit the streets!

**Shawna, We both knew he had plans for this evening,
but he didn't tell me anything either.**

The agencies have most of the details through surveillance, But we don't know
where or what time...
That information is only known by a very few at the top of his organization!
And most likely... You!

Me..??? Why don't you just follow him tonight.. ?

Yeah, right... He's wayy to clever for that!
If that were the case, hell we would have had him years ago..

So what does all of this has to do with Zephyr?

Zephyr is actually a two part situation for Marquise...
On one hand, Zeph is a part of the board of director that's preventing Marquise from
obtaining that local YMCA he wants for his organization's headquarters..

But that 'Y' does so much for the kids… Everybody knows that!

The other part is, from way back in the day… when Zephyr's cousins
murdered Marquise's younger brother in a gang related situation.

I didn't know Zeph was a gang banger..!

He wasn't, some of his friends and relatives were, Zeph was always into sports and
family, just a normal kid growing up in this abnormal world.

**So you're saying Marquise is bringing Zephyr down because of what his family
did to his brother?**

Yes, and also, the shoe endorsements!!

What?

Nike cancelled Marquise's 'Thug Style' brand because of them launching
the new 'Zephyr Fire' series…

Really?? All This is Just Over shoes??

JUST over Shoes…??
You're talking upwards of $25 million a year Marquise stands to lose
because of losing his endorsements…

So he wants Zeph to understand, what it feels like..?

Well, yeah, pretty much!

Wow… that's incredible!!

So Jazz… with all that being said, talk to me… Where's that buy at tonight??

I don't know... Shawna..

Com'on Jazz don't give me that Shit... Where's the buy at Tonight..?

I was never told anything about this...

Stop it, I know you're LYING!
You know... you were under surveillance too!!

Me? ... What, I was??

Yes, so don't try to Bullshit Me!!

I Don't Know!!...

Where at tonight... OR ... I put your Ass back out there on the streets...
I'm sure Marquise's people will be happy to stop and give you a ride!
Now WHAT's IT GONNA BE JAZZ...??

I don't know, ... I mean I'm not sure...

Not SURE..??

I think... It's the code to the Bentley's security...?

What's that..?

The security code to the Bentley SUV Is actually... the address, of the... Y-M-C-A!

Are you SERIOUS..??

Team..., guys did you get that..?
Its going down tonight at the YMCA... That's Right..
Of All places... The YMCA..!!

TO BE CONTINUED

Adam Dumars (ESPN Reporter) = Bd Brn   Grace Seavers (Private Inv.) = Lt Blu

---

Candi Rae Hasara (Daughter) = **Bd Blue**   **(Receptionist) = Bd Tan**

(While having lunch...)
Okay Adam, We know Marquise is behind this video ordeal, and I'm sure that and the assault allegations together are a part of a larger scheme too.

But we don't really know if he's behind the assault claims.

But I've been a detective long enough to know how to read my gut instincts

I really doubt that those allegations are true..

And that's what my instincts are telling me..

But I'm sure Marquise has ways of disconnecting himself from situations
so that he can go undetected

But what does Marquise stand to gain by bringing Zephyr down?

Good question... Let's go ask Marquise!!

**What.. Oh right, Like he's just going to say,
"Hey yeah, I did it because of..."**

You never know, maybe he likes bragging!

(Just then Grace's phone rings..)
Hello, Grace Seavers...

**Hi Grace, this is Candi Rae Hasara, my dad gave me your card and...
you wanted to speak to me?**

Yes, thanks for calling...

I am doing an investigation and had a few questions for you.

Like what? What are you investigating?

I'm working on behalf of Mr. Parker, basically I was hired to get to the bottom of the allegations against him.

Yes, I knew you were coming onboard, what can I do to help?

First of all, I wanted to know, in the video it showed you there with Mr. Parker...

Huh... What, what video..? AND where??

Oh you don't know about the video...

No! What's going on?

There's a video that surfaced... It shows Zephyr causing problems and starting trouble in a bar, and you were there with him!

Yes I was, but Zephyr wasn't the one starting the problems, it was those gang bangers starting stuff with Zeph!!

So you haven't seen the YouTube video yet?

**Give me a few minutes... I'm going to look it up!
OH My God, that is NOT how things happened!!**

Oh Really, How did it happen?

**Those guys are the ones that started that, somehow,
someone has made it look like Zeph was in the wrong, yes I was there,
and what you see on that video did not happen like that!**

And that's my next question... Why were you and Mr. Parker there at that location in the first place?

*We were meeting a couple of friends for a little something to eat,
I had no idea who frequents that place...*

I see, so it was just random that you were there?

**Yes!... well, no... not really...
It was actually suggested by my friends Jazlyn and Shawna...**

Jazlyn Summers?

Yes!

I see... and Who's Shawna?

Shawna Smith... She's an old friend also, she's an Attny... Special Counsel for the local YMCA..

So how did you end up there at the bar With.. Mr. Parker?

Jazz and I went to pick up Shawna at her office, and Zeph..., Mr. Parker was there meeting with his Attny...

*Wait, so what you're saying is...
Mr. Parker's Attny is in the same office as Ms. Smith...
and Ms. Smith is friends with Jazlyn Summers, and Jazlyn is the girlfriend of...
Marquise Brimson..??*

Oh my God... Yes!!

And let me guess, Brimson also owns the bar where all this took place at...?

**Yes, yes he does... 'De OG's Pound'..!
Could this be a coincidence..?**

*I seriously doubt it... my gut instinct!
I think we may need to pay Ms. Smith a visit, where's her office located?*

I'll text you the address..

Great, hey Candi Rae... Thanks for the chat!
You have been so helpful...

No problem Grace, if there's anything else...

If so I have your number in my phone...

Okay, Good luck Grace..

Take care Candi...

Wow, This is getting deep!
It's becoming clearer as a setup, but still the question of the day remains, Why?

It's incredible!!
So do you have that address yet?

Got it ...
Let's go speak to Ms. Shawna, if you thought getting a straight answer from the gang
bangers was tough, we now have to go question an Attny...!

Never thought about it that way...
Kinda like outta the pan, into the fire!

Yeah, those two would make good bed fellows... Lol

HEYY... I wonder??

What's that?

A guy like Marquise... women kinda go for the bad boy type...
Do you think that they could be... lovers as well?

Mmm... It probably would be in his best interest to keep her close!

Oh heck, they all could be lovers...

Let's go and see what Ms. Shawna has to inject into the mix!

You got it...

(A little while later, they pull into the driveway of the Attny's office building...)

Wow! Nice place!

Yeah, Someone looks very successful...

Valet parking .. At your Attny's office..!
Wow, I can't imagine what her retainer and fees looks like!

It's one of those situations where, if you have to ask, you can't afford it!!

... And that's why I ask..!

Com'on, let's go up!... (smile)

(As they enter the lobby area)

Whoa.. is this the lobby or the VIP Lounge?

My God... it's Both..!
Let's check with the receptionist...

Hi, May I help you?

Yes, we're here to see an Attny, a Ms. Shawna Smith.

I'm sorry, Ms. Smith is out of the office for the rest of the day...

Darn...

I'm sorry, but did you have an appointment?

No.. I thought I'd just drop by..

Well maybe we have someone else here who can be of service to you?
What area of legal services may you be interested in?

Mmm... Excuse me, one second please...

{If Zephyr's Attny is in this office as well as Shawna, what are the chances of those two
female accusers' Attny being in the building also?}

{No way... How can we find out?
And what would that actually prove?}

{If she is in here, it helps establish the foundation of a conspiracy,
and it also means that IF and WHEN,
Mr. Parker has to rely on his legal team... he's screwed..!!}

{Yeah, so how do we find out?}

{Simple, let's just ask the receptionist... She seems nice!}

{Ok Grace, Let's do it...}

Excuse me...

Yes, how can I help you?

There was a press conference this morning, it was on the news,
Did you happen to catch it?

No ma'am I'm sry.. I've been here since very early.. What was it pertaining to?

Oh it was about a couple of women.. I think their Attny is here in this office as well...

Well what's the Attny's name?

I'm not sure...

Okay, Let me look up the news online here..
and checking the article for the, Attny's name...

And here it is... Oh my gosh...!

What?

This Attny, she used to be apart of this law group,
but something happened...
And now she's no longer here!

What happened?

I can't say.. But, so... um, is there anything else I can help you with?

Yes... Which Attny here is the counsel for Mr. Dexter Lee Parker?

That's what this article is about... Ok ma'am... Who are you?

I'm Grace Seavers, Private Investigator.. and this is Adam...
We have some questions for the Attny of Mr. Parker, can we see him?

I'm sry Mr. Parkers Attny is out of the office as well..
But you can leave a message for him.

When will he return?

Oh Mr. Dumars, he may not be back for the rest of the day also...

You know my name??

Oh yeah...!
My boyfriend and I watch College and Pro Football together!!
We Love ESPN... and Sport Center!!

Super nice.. Thx..!!

I love watching the football highlights,
and you hear that voice say... "He-May-Go-All-The-Way!" ... Awesome stuff..!

Hehe well ... that wasn't me, but yeah,... good stuff..!
So tell me, Zeph's Attny, what's his name again?

Karson..

Great, so what's the big issues going on with Zephyr?

What do you mean?

You're into sports, you're right here at the forefront of it all..
This is like... ground zero!

Yeah.. You won't believe what goes on here..

Oh I bet.. I had a 4 hour conversation with Tom Brady once that started with
those same exact words!

Oh wow, 4 hours with Tom..!!

Oh yeah, was really a cool dude...

Oh my gosh, what a dream job you have!!

Yeah... Say, you wanna meet him?

Get real...!!

I swear.. Really!

Let me guess, give you some information, you promise to introduce Tom...

Shucks, I wish!!
Do you know how much stuff I could get in life if that were possible..! Lol

Oh my gosh Mr. Dumars... You're a trip!.. (smile)

Well at least I did make you smile!

That you did... Okay hey, here's a freebee...

What's that??

I'm going to tell you this, and you didn't hear it from me...
Then you two, you have to leave this office...

What's up?

I knew something terrible was going to take place awhile ago but
I didn't know what, cause... um..

Go on...

Well, It was a big argument in the conference room one day...
Zephyr's Attny, Karson... that 'Still' works here.

And the Attny for those female accusers,
that 'Used' to work here,
Her name is Dallas..!
Anyway, they are in fact, ... {Brother and Sister}

TO BE CONTINUED

Adam Dumars (ESPN reporter) = Brn   Grace Seavers (Private Inv.) = Lt Blu

---

Hustle Man (Bartender) = Bold Tan   **Marquise Brimson (Ex Baller, OG) = Dk Grn**

Shawna Smith (Attny/Fed. Agent) = Purple   **Jazlyn S. (Marquise's Girlfriend) = Org**

Candi Rae Hasara (Daughter) = Bold Blue   Zephyr Parker (Baller) = Red

---

(Grace and Adam in the car together...)

So is that legal... is that okay in the judicial system to allow siblings to be as opposing counsel in a court case?

I'm not sure, but I can imagine in Zephyr case, under these circumstances, it's probably not going to be a good thing!

But now at the same time, it does tie in the female accusers to Marquise through the Attny trail...

That's probably what the big blow up in the conference room was about somehow...

Yeah, I would bet it was a part of it too...

Hey great work on getting the info from the receptionist, that was smooth...

Thanks, not bad yourself...
I've been watching you all day Grace, gotta tell you...
You're the one that has a unique talent, now that's mind blowing ... Awesome!

Aww... Thanks!

I mean really, you've only been in town for what, maybe 6 or 7 hours...?
And look at all that you've uncovered...

We've uncovered... Adam!

Yeah, true... We have done a really good job together..

Yes, But we're still not done yet, and we still don't know why Zeph's a target...

If we want to know that answer, you know where we need to go..?

Yeah I guess it's the one place left to go...

Time to go dance with the Devil...

No, Not yet, he's too big and powerful to just run up on him without a true plan.

Okay, but what angle do you take with a guy like that?

Well, everyone there may recognize you from tv anyway...

Maybe that's a positive or good thing... Maybe we can use that..

Yeah, Let me think... Let me think...
Mmmmm YES!... I got it...

Okay how's it going to go down?

You watch too much Law and Order...
Anyway, we can use your tv notoriety...

How's that?

We can go there as to do an interview with some of the people that may have witnessed Zephyr's ordeal...

I see, so basically I can go play.. Me!

Yes, and I will be like your... production assistant, person, staff or something...

How's about you just use your cellphone to video me doing some interviews...

No real camera?

No, the phone will do, just hold it steady and look professional...
And Grace..

Yes?

Yeah, I think you're awesome!

You know that's twice you've told me that in a matter of 5 minutes!
... But who's counting... (smile)

So are you about ready Grace?

Yeah Adam, let's go to that dance you were talking about...

See, You do have a sense of humor!

(As they arrive at the location of the restaurant/bar, 'De OG's Pound'...)

Oh okay, this place isn't that intimidating at all..

Adam, it's a restaurant..!

Yeah, from the video you would think you're entering a biker bar

Well remember, Candi said the video was altered to look a certain way.

"C'est la Vie"... Such is Life..
Okay, where do we start?

Well let's head to the bar, you've seen the movies, the bartenders are always
the ones that have the info...

Hey Boss, what can I get for you?

Hey guy... What's up..
So um, do you know who I am?

No, is this a game you wanna play or you wanna order a drink?

Neither, I'm Adam Dumars, Sports reporter..
Doing a lil follow up on the video that surfaced from here with Zephyr

Sounds like you DO wanna drink... But, it does comes with a hefty tip in the end!

Well ok then, Cool... Capt. & Coke... for me!

And for the Lady?

Grace, what'll you have?

White wine... Please..

Thank you, Coming up...

See, not a biker bar..

I know, but I do get the feeling that we're being watched!

I'm sure... you look fantastic, not to mention you walked in the place like you're the new sheriff in town!

Old habits are hard to die...

I bet, you were probably a real bad ass as a cop..

Being a cop was great...

What happened?

I guess I lost the desire to follow the system's directions...

Really. How come?

When my partner was killed in the line of duty, I wanted to get revenge...
but was ordered to let it go, said I was to close too the victim...

And then what did you do?

I quit... That was the only way to seek the proper justice for my partner!

What happened after that?

Well, to make a long story short, ... I did what I do best!

**Here you go, White wine for the lady,
and a Captain & Coke for Mr. Sports Center...**

Funny... I Thought you Knew..!!

So what is it you wanna know?

**Oh wait first, let's do it like this...
I'm going to put the tip bucket right here, so every time you feel the need
for an answer remember,... 'baby needs a new pair a shoes'..!!**

What??

Just put the tip money in the bucket...!

Okay, Why would Zephyr come in here to start trouble?

**Honestly, I don't think he came here to start anything,
but sometimes trouble can find you..**

Had he been here before causing problems?

He, you forgot something... the bucket!

Dang.. Ok

No, I hadn't seen him up in here before... Zeph's family an crew are from the east side,
years ago, he had better not shown up in here...
he would've been carried out...

Why's that?

Bucket...

Oh.. the bucket!... Ok, Why's that?

Street gang stuff.. Years ago, Marquise and his brotha were hanging out,
just chillin playing dominos, or whatever...

And some of them Eastside Mafia boys did a drive by...
they took out Marquise's brother... Damn shame too!

During those days, was Zeph a part of that gang?

No,... but you did forgot the bucket again...

Awww... here, here's all the cash I have!!

I take credit and debit cards...

Oh my gosh... Okay, here's the big money question...
Why is Marquise trying to bring down Zephyr...??

That's a huge tip question!!... Was that Visa or MasterCard?

To the point...

First of all the shoe contracts... Marquise got dropped because of Zeph...

That's it, this is about shoes??

It's a combination of things.., then there's the payback for his brother...

Still seems as though something's missing, it all still doesn't add up...

There's some more big stuff going on... too!

What's that??

I wish I knew... my rent is due soon!!

Thanks man, appreciate it... You've been helpful...
Expensive, but helpful..!

Good service costs... Boss!

Speaking of that, is Marquise around?

Naa man, he only comes around when he needs too...

Okay.. Well I guess we better get rolling Grace..

Yeah, are you about ready?

Yeah..

So are you ready to settle your tab now?

What? More money, it's expensive in here..

You knew where you were at when you walked through the door...

Let's get out of here, almost $200 bucks, and we didn't even have anything to eat...

Let's go Adam...

Hey, Come back soon... Hell, my electric is due in a few weeks! (smile)

Yeah Adam, I feel there's something else missing too, just can't quite put my finger on it...

We've actually never spoken to most of the people that we were looking for...

I know, and still look what we've uncovered

What's your next direction?

I'm thinking about going to talk to my Boss-man!

Zephyr?

Yes, ... Mr. Parker indeed!!

Yeah, we probably should have started there... Ok,... Let's do it!

Yo Marquise, this 'Hustle Man' down at the bar...

What's up Hustle, whatcha got for me?

Hey these people came thru here asking a lot of questions...

Oh yeah... My girl over at the lawyer's office...
She said the same ones were over there not long ago...

Shawna's office?

yeah...

What did they wanna know?

Asking about you and ya boy Zeph...

Did they ask about tonight?

Naa, I don't think they know about tonight, I threw it out there
that something big was up, but they didn't bite!

Maybe they already know, but just playing dumb...
Can't take no chances... Okay, change of plans...

Tell everybody to swing by the bar, we need to talk...
I'll get back to you soon... Later

Okay Jazz, we have to go and set up the sting... You're going to remain here in the command center...

When do I get to go home? Am I under arrest?

It depends on how things turnout...
Worst case scenario, Hell, you may not be able to go home for 5 to 10 years!

OH MY GOD...! (crying)

Stop crying, you knew that shit was wrong that you were doing,
and the crowds you were hanging with...
Now put on your big girl panties and deal with it...

Shawnaaa...! (crying)

Jazz, we're heading out early, Special Agent Buckner is in charge here, she and her crew
are here to protect YOU, so just sit there, And don't try Anything Stupid..!!

Com'on guys,... We're Out..!

Wow, look at this place... You know, these ball players amaze me at their style
and taste for the finer things in life!!

I know, I do have one of the greatest jobs in the world where I get to rub elbows with some of the top athletes in the world... I'm always in awe..!!

Oh but Adam, you're one of the top in the world yourself...
Heck you're as much of a celebrity as these top pro ballers are...!

Really, oh thanks Grace!

And... you're a real guy.. I like that in you..! (smile)

Oh well... (smile).. Thank You!!

Com'on, let's go talk to Mr. Parker!!

...Your Boss-man!!

Hehe... Yeah... Which I haven't even met yet...

*(They ring the doorbell, and Candi Rae answers the front door...
wearing only an oversized men's tee-shirt)*
Hi... Wait, What... Candi Rae..??

Yes..?

What are you doing here?

What?... Who are you??

Sorry, I'm Grace Seavers... PI, and this is Adam Dumars, Investigative Reporter!!

Oh... Yeah..

Sry, It was just a little surprising to see you here...
And to be dressed so.. Um... well, Anyway... We're here to see Mr. Parker...

Oh yes!!, excuse me... Com'on in... I'll go get him!

Well Surprise, Surprise!

Right, I don't know why we should be shocked...

Heyy Adam Dumars!... And you must be the lovely Ms. Grace!!

Grace Seavers... Yes, Nice to finally meet you!

Yeah, same here.. So my agent told me all about you!
And how has Adam been treating you..?

Oh Adam, he's been very instrumental at getting the facts!!

Don't listen to her... Man, she's the one, she's awesome..!!

So how's it going? Have you found out anything yet?

Oh boy did we..? So where do you want us to start?

At the part where you decided to come here...!

Okay, here it is... Basically, We have Marquise Brimson as the prime suspect behind the dealing that has lead to your job dismissal, and to you losing your contract endorsements...

What's the reasons why... I can imagine a long time ago things were really bad between the rival gangs, but we were kids then...
An I actually never really had anything to do with it all...
So why now?

Now THAT's the million dollar question...!!

And that's why,... we're here...!!

Think, what else is it that you may have, that Brimson may wanna take away?

Heck, he's taken the job, the endorsements, I guess the charities are the
only thing left...

What charities?

The homeless food banks, the free medical plaza, the free daycare...
at the YMCA, the free elderly transportation, and meals programs...
Well..., that's about all...

WHAT..!! Really?? That's about all..??

But come to think about it, that YMCA has become a little contested.

Huh, what do you mean?

I'm on the board of directors, and my word becomes the final say so...

That sounds different than the way most are operated...

Oh it is... this place is truly special..
In many ways and that's why I'd never vote to close it, or to sell the property!!

WAIT!... OMG!... So is that what this is all about..??
and that's why Ms. Shawna is needed so much...!!
To get the property of which the "Y" sits on..??

REALLY...!!
And destroy my life over WHAT..??
A Building and Property?
Oh my God... I can't... I can't believe it...!

Calm down... I can understand how disheartening this must be...

NOW WHAT, NOW WHAT GRACE...??

It has to be a really good reason why that location is so important to destroy
someone's life over...

No, I'm sure there is never any good reason to destroy someone's life...
Where is that property located..?

It's near downtown...

I wanna see it.. I wanna go see the area also...

I'll go with you guys... I have the keys to the front door,
we can go inside and check it out...

Let me change clothes, and let Candi know we're riding out...

(As Grace, Adam, and Zephyr head to the YMCA..!!
...Back at the 'De OG's Pound'... the gang's meeting is already in progress)

Yeah, we got there and the place was locked up, but the Bentley was there...
We brought it back, un-scratched...!!

So still no signs of Jazlyn..?

Nope!

And so what about Shawna, has anyone heard from her either..??

We checked their offices and their cribs... not a word...

Okay, I've tried too.... Something is definitely not right... here's the deal...

Since Jazz knows the buy spot, I truly believe she won't tell the proper location
if questioned... BUT, we can't take any chances that she won't...

So we'll have to change location for the weapons buy tonight...

But everything is already set up...
So You don't like the warehouse location anymore?

Nope, not anymore... Those weapons are too important, and wayy too valuable for something to go wrong!!

So with that being said, we'll have extra fire power on our side just incase, some serious fire power too..!!

So where do you think we should change the location to..?

To the one place where no one would ever think...

 "The YMCA"..!!

WILL BE CONTINUED

THE END ... ZONE

THE END OF SEASON ONE!
"THE OFFSEASON"

COACH 'EM UP! ™

Is a Registered Trademark

CREDITS:
Cover illustration
Copyright 2020/2021 Jerome DeBose

Cover Design Illustrations by:
Matt Davies for Very Much So.agency
Manchester, UK

Book Design and production by:
Jerome DeBose

Research Assistant
Elaine S.

Book Editing by:
Margaret Joyce

Photography:
Steven Le, TheePhotoNinja.com

DISCLAIMER:
This is a work of fiction!
Names and characters, businesses, places, events, locales, and incidents are either the products of the author's imagination or used in a fictitious manner.
Any resemblance to actual persons, living or dead, or actual events is purely coincidental.

All cast Illustrations are
Computer generated (CGI) photo depictions.
No copyright infringements intended

The Historical YMCA, St. Petersburg, Florida
www.TheEdwardStPete.com

Book Ordering information: www.CoachEmUpSeries.com

Copyright Office registration number: TXu 2-271-235
ISBN: 979-8-987-9858-1-6

2021 First Edition
Conceived, Written and Made in the USA

Jerome grew up in an era of the
'Last of the Big Families',
with a household of Father, Mother,
five brothers and three sisters.

He is the second youngest, which is where he gives
credit to the entire family for the
True family values learned.

He was able to watch and learn from the
accomplishments of his older siblings…
and also from the mistakes.

But he still had his own curiosity to live life,
and to learn from some of his own mistakes, as well.

After college he started his professional engineering career at the age of 20 in the recording industry,
Jerome was bitten by the "Entertainment bug" and that would last a lifetime.

He has managed vocal artists and musicians, produced recorded music, live shows
and has produced and directed music videos during his extensive career.

And it was sometime during his time on set as an extra for a major motion picture,
and a cameo appearance in one of his music videos productions that the "Acting bug" took hold!

After enrolling in professional acting classes,
along with acting out live scene performances using the Eric Morris theories and techniques,
Jerome began to refine his craft, but these classes came to an abrupt halt in early 2020 when
the Coronavirus pandemic shutdown the world.

Still being the behind the scene person that has always loved the great stories of music and songs,
Jerome has found a new passion for writing the stories of dramatic scenes!

COACH 'EM UP! ™

Is his first project manifested of and from the Life and Times of which we now Live in…
May God Bless!